Angela
Bewick

Illustrated by
Sabrina Sachiko Niebler

Bob,
the
Apple

FriesenPress

Suite 300 - 990 Fort St
Victoria, BC, V8V 3K2
Canada

www.friesenpress.com

www.angelabewick.com

Illustrations by Sabrina Sachiko Niebler

ISBN
978-1-5255-9719-0 (Hardcover)
978-1-5255-9718-3 (Paperback)
978-1-5255-9720-6 (eBook)

1. JUVENILE FICTION, NATURE & THE NATURAL WORLD

Distributed to the trade by The Ingram Book Company

Thank you to my parents for the strong roots to grow from and to my beloved and our babies for the branches to swing upon.
This book is dedicated to you, dear reader and to the beautiful planet we share.

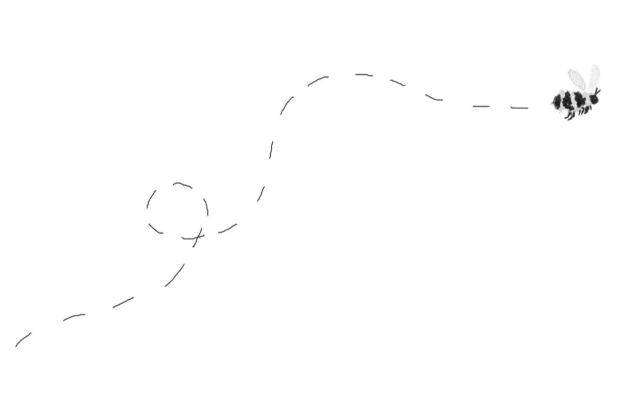

Bob was an apple.

He lived on the branch of a large tree in a small grove behind a small house.

There was nothing that made
Bob happier than to hang out
in the summer sun on the
branch of his tree,

with all his
brothers and sisters,
being fed by their mother,
the Earth. This was home.

By autumn, things were beginning to change for Bob and his siblings.

Soon, Bob began to notice that his brothers and sisters were being picked. Some were even falling from the tree straight to the ground on their own!

I want to be part of an apple pie!

This made Bob feel VERY uncomfortable. Would he have to leave the tree too? Would he be the only apple left? What was going to happen to him?!

Bob asked his father,
"Papa, do you think that I
could stay with you
forever?" His father smiled
a kind smile, the way trees
do, and Bob continued.
"I could keep you company in
the winter and in the
springtime, I could help
with the new buds. I could
teach them how to be apples."

His father held him close in that special tree kind of way.

"Bob, why do you want to stay with me forever?
Forever is a long time."

"I'm scared, Papa," said Bob.

"What are you scared of?" his father asked kindly.

"I'm scared of growing up," Bob replied.

The old tree took a deep breath.
"Bob, did you know that once I was an apple?"

"You were? What happened? How did you become such
a great and enormous tree?" Bob exclaimed.

His father replied, "Well, when the time was right, I was picked and most of me was eaten. The core that was left held my seeds. When the sun's heat was just right and I had enough water and enough soil, my seeds sprouted open and I began to grow into a tree. I'm very big because I've been growing for a long, long time."

Bob was amazed by this news.
"You mean I'll grow into a tree someday?"

"Not every seed will become a tree; seeds can become many things," his father replied. "But unless the seed is exposed, it has no chance. So you see, Bob, there's no reason to be afraid. You can trust in Mother Nature."

One warm and sunny September morning,
a robin landed on the tree and Bob asked,
"Robin, what do you want to be
when you grow up?"

"I'm it! I'm a robin and I'm the best robin I know."

"But aren't you worried about tomorrow, about the winter coming?" Bob asked.

"No! Why worry about tomorrow when a beautiful day is here now? You're an apple, enjoy being an apple, someday you'll be something else. It's like my grandma always said, 'You can't make a robin without breaking an egg.'"

It's not always easy to change your mind, but after some time, Bob didn't feel afraid anymore.

"Papa, it's okay for you to let
me go when the time is right,"
he said calmly.

His father smiled, "It's not me
who lets go of you, Bob. It's you
who lets go of me."

Granny Jean's Apple Crisp

This is my Granny Jean's recipe for Apple Crisp and it's delicious! Apples are one of the most nutritious foods we can eat. They are high in vitamin C, antioxidant-rich and contain a good amount of fibre, which is very important in helping our bodies eliminate waste. Fibre is the main food for the helpful bugs in our intestines which helps us to stay healthy! The fibre is mostly in the skins of apples, so be sure to munch on the skins if you chose to peel them. Did you know there are over 7,500 varieties of apples in the world? You can try this recipe with different types of apples and see which one you like best!

My favourite is organic apples that were grown close to where I live. Kids – make sure you have an adult help you so you stay safe in the kitchen. Have fun!

4 cups sliced apples (you can peel them if you like, but you can also keep the skin on!)
1 cup of berries (or an extra cup of apples!)
1 tbsp lemon juice
1/3 cup flour (or gluten-free flour)
1 cup quick-cooking rolled oats
½ - ¾ cup sugar (I use coconut sugar or Sucanat - natural unrefined sugar cane powder - but you can use brown sugar if you prefer)
½ tsp salt (optional)
½ -1 tsp cinnamon
1/3 cup melted butter (or coconut oil for a vegan option)
1 dash of love and a sprinkle of gratitude

Preheat oven to 375°F
Place fruit in slightly greased 9x13" pan.
Sprinkle fruit with lemon juice.
Combine dry ingredients in bowl.
Add melted butter to dry ingredient bowl and add sugar.
Mix until crumbly.
Sprinkle mixture on top of fruit and spread evenly.
Bake at 375°F for 30 minutes or until fruit is done.
Serve topped with cream of your choice.

About the Author and Illustrator

Angela Bewick is a nutrition coach, writer and lover of life. She got the idea for *Bob, The Apple* when her kids asked her over and over and over again for another bedtime story and when she couldn't think of anything, her son said "tell us a story about an apple!" When she saw Sachiko's drawings, she knew that she had to make the story into a book and here you are reading it! This is her first book. She lives in Calgary with her husband and two children. Her favourite way to eat apples is straight from the tree or in her mom/grandma's apple crisp! Check out www.angelabewick.com to learn more about her work.

Sabrina Sachiko Niebler is a weaver and creative residing in Vancouver, BC. She is a graduate of the Alberta University of the Arts and loves a good, crisp apple! You will often find her at her loom, walking in the rain, or cradling her big cat Mo.

Lightning Source UK Ltd.
Milton Keynes UK
UKHW050337020622
403869UK00007B/92